This edition is based on a book published in Hebrew under the title *Veaz Hatzav Banah Lo Bayit* by Avner Katz, © 1979.

Tortoise Solves a Problem Copyright © 1993 by Avner Katz   Printed in the U.S.A.
All rights reserved. Typography by Elynn Cohen 1 2 3 4 5 6 7 8 9 10 ❖
First Edition Library of Congress Cataloging-in-Publication Data Katz, Avner.   Tortoise
solves a problem / Avner Katz.   p.   cm "Willa Perlman books."   Summary: In
the days before tortoises had shells, one talented young tortoise sets out to design the
perfect house for his fellow crawlers.   ISBN 0-06-020798-1. — ISBN 0-06-020799-X (lib.
bdg.)   [1. Turtles—Fiction.   2. Dwellings—Fiction.]   I. Title. PZ7.K1567To   1993
[E]—dc20   91-32503   CIP AC

TORTOISE
SOLVES
A PROBLEM

AVNER KATZ

Willa Perlman Books
An Imprint of HarperCollinsPublishers

There was a time—you may even have already heard about it—when the tortoise didn't have a house. He didn't have any shelter from the fierce sun beating down on his back . . .

. . . or the cold rain pelting down on his head. He was always out, and never in.

Sometimes, when the sun's heat was very great, the tortoise had to walk such a long way to find shade that his feet became sore and burned. And although he tried not to feel sorry for himself, there were days when he did.

He felt sorriest for himself when the other animals, who all had snug, cozy homes to go to, taunted him. It was a hard life being a tortoise, then.

Life was so difficult for tortoises everywhere that the Three Wisest Tortoises in the land put their heads together to come up with a plan. The tortoises needed a house. But what kind of house would be most suitable?

After a lengthy discussion it was agreed that they must find a
tortoise clever enough to design a tortoise house. And so they set
off, prepared to search high and low, far and wide.

Fortunately, they had to search only high and low before coming across a young tortoise who had an obvious gift for building. He could put one block on top of another, and another on top of that, until he'd made a pile of blocks that didn't fall down—even when a butterfly landed on it!

The Three Wisest Tortoises knew in an instant that they had found the one to solve the tortoise housing problem. But first he would have to go and learn from master builders all over the world. So they helped him pack and sent him on his way.

After a few years of study the young tortoise returned to a warm welcome. The Three Wisest Tortoises were delighted to hear that he was bursting with ideas for the tortoise house.

But he had so many ideas . . .

. . . he didn't know where to begin.

It was nearly a year later that the young tortoise invited the Three Wisest Tortoises to come and see the house that he had built.

"Look at its height, its width, its depth!" he exclaimed proudly. "And look, the top turns with the sun and casts a shadow at every point of the compass."

"The top is certainly something," said the Three Wisest Tortoises, "even though a sudden wind could blow it off. But it's not a house. Nobody, least of all a tortoise, could *live* in that."

After another year had passed, the young tortoise invited the Three Wisest Tortoises to come again to see the new house he'd built.

"Have you ever seen chimneys like this before? I can change the color of the smoke just with the touch of a button!"

"The chimneys are fantastic," said the Three Wisest Tortoises. "Marvelous. But it's not a house. Nobody, least of all a tortoise, could *live* in that."

"Back to the drawing board," said the young tortoise cheerfully.

And, the following year, he invited the Three Wisest Tortoises to come again to see the new house he'd built.

"I've tried to build something full of light, color, and air," he said.

"And you've done it," the Three Wisest Tortoises acknowledged. "But it's not a house. Nobody, least of all a tortoise, could *live* in that."

And they left without even saying good-bye.

One more year had passed when the young tortoise came to the Three Wisest Tortoises and said, "You must come and see what I've built this time. I've really surpassed myself. It's out of this world!"

But the Three Wisest Tortoises shook their heads. "Not this time," they said. "We're growing old, and we're tired of traveling to and fro to see your ridiculous contraptions. If you want to show us a new tortoise house, you must bring it to us."

And they sent him away without saying good-bye.

The poor young tortoise was very hurt and saddened by their words. He built himself a hill a long way off and climbed up on top of it to think. And there he thought, and he asked himself over and over again, "Where did I go wrong?"

Then, all of a sudden, he understood and shouted, "Eureka!"—which means "I have found it!" And then he shouted "I have found it!"—which means "Eureka!"

Immediately, so as not to waste a moment more, he measured his height . . .

. . . the width of his chest, and the length of his legs.

And then he sat down at his drawing board to produce his final plan.

When he went to see the Three Wisest Tortoises again, he was carrying something rather unusual on his back.

"What's that?" they asked.

"It's my house," replied the young tortoise. "From now on all tortoises will carry their houses on their backs. The tortoise housing problem is solved."

"Bravo!" shouted the Three Wisest Tortoises—which means "Well done!" And then they shouted "Well done!"—which means "Bravo!" They shook him warmly by the hand, patted him—gently—on his house, and then congratulated themselves on having chosen him to design the tortoise house in the first place.

The celebrations went on until the next day. Glasses were raised—and so was the young tortoise—as they sang "For He's a Jolly Good Fellow!" And within two weeks, all the tortoises throughout the land had houses on their backs to shelter them from the hot sun and cold rain.

There was one snag, however. The tortoises' new houses didn't have a bit of extra room for a friend to come in and visit. This was a pity, but by the time the tortoises realized the problem, a million years, if not two, had gone by, and it was a little too late for design changes.